First Edition
10 9 8 7 6 5 4 3 2 1
ISBN 978-1-4231-8655-7
F322-8368-0-14234
Library of Congress Control Number: 2014939786
Printed in the USA
For more Disney Press fun, visit www.disneybooks.com

Sofia
the First

The
Curse of
Princess
Ivy

Written by

Craig Gerber and Catherine Hapka

Based on an episode by

Erica Rothschild

Illustrated by

Grace Lee

DISNEP PRESS

New York • Los Angeles

I'm Sofia.

When I became a

princess,

my new dad, King Roland, gave me the
Amulet of Avalor.

It gives me the power to talk to animals.

Nobody is supposed to know about that.
But one day Amber overhears me
talking to Clover.

"You looked like you understood
what Clover was saying!
What's going on?"
Amber asks.

Even though I'm not
supposed to tell **anyone** about
the amulet's powers, I can't lie to Amber.
So I tell her the truth: the amulet is magical.
It even calls princesses when I need them.

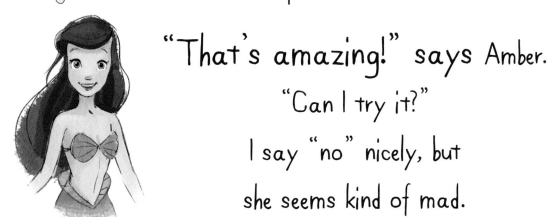

"That's amazing!" says Amber.
"Can I try it?"
I say "no" nicely, but
she seems kind of mad.

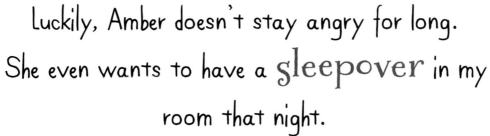

Luckily, Amber doesn't stay angry for long.
She even wants to have a sleepover in my
room that night.

I'm glad she isn't holding a grudge.
We end up having a great time!

But when I wake up the
next morning, Amber is gone—
and so is my amulet!
Could Amber have taken it?

I search everywhere and finally find Amber in the garden.

She's wearing my amulet!

"I just wanted a turn," she says.

Then she wishes for the amulet to bring her a princess.

It starts to glow . . .

...and a **princess** appears!

Amber is **excited,** but I'm confused.
"Usually the amulet only sends princesses when
I'm in trouble or need help," I tell Amber.
I don't recognize this princess. Who is she?

"I'm Princess Ivy," she says. "I'm here to take over your kingdom, and without your magic amulet, you can't stop me!" Suddenly, one of her black-and-white butterflies grabs the amulet.

"Give that **back**!"
I cry.

I call a guard to stop Ivy, but she stuns him with a magical dragonfly. "Where am I?" he asks.

Oh, no!

Ivy's dragonfly took away his memory!

"I'll be back for the crown after I destroy the amulet," Ivy says. "You can't destroy it!" I cry.

"Oh, I can, and I will," she says, rushing off.

"How was I supposed to know the amulet
would summon an **evil** princess?" Amber asks.
Then I remember the rules of the amulet:

With each deed performed,
for better or worse, a power is
granted, a blessing—or curse.

"You stole the amulet, so it must have
cursed you by bringing Ivy here,"
I tell her.

We need help,
so we go find Mr. Cedric.
He says only the flame of
Everburn the Dragon can harm
my amulet. "Everburn lives atop
the Blazing Palisades. Nobody
else knows of him except us."
Then I hear a flutter.
Oh, no—one of Ivy's
butterflies
heard what Cedric said!

We chase the butterfly, but we can't stop it from telling Ivy about Everburn. Once she knows, she flies off to find him, leaving her butterflies to turn Enchancia **black and white!**

We have to stop her!
"Maybe if we save the amulet,
the curse will be broken!" I say.
We fly to the Blazing Palisades
and land beside Ivy's coach.

"Wait," Amber says.
"We have to climb all the way up there?"
"Yes, Amber. We do," I tell her, leading
the way up the steep trail.
I hope we're not
too late. . . .

Finally, we reach the caves near the top.
We look for Everburn but we don't see him.
We don't see Ivy, either, but I'm sure
she's here somewhere. . . .

Suddenly, we hear a voice sing,

"Hellooooooo!"

Four dragons step into view.
They seem friendly, so I ask
where we can find Everburn.

"We'd be **happy** to tell you,"
says one dragon.
"Right after the show!" adds another.

We try to explain that
we're in a hurry, but they're already
starting to sing.

The dragons finally finish their
song and tell us where to go.
But when we find Everburn's
cave, Princess Ivy is already
there—and Everburn is about
to melt the amulet!

In a flash, Cedric makes a
flock of birds appear to distract Ivy.

Amber grabs the amulet
and tosses it to me.
But that doesn't break the curse.
Ivy is still here!

She zaps Cedric
with a dragonfly so
he loses his memory.
Then she comes after us!

As we're running away,
we fall into a deep pit.
Luckily, Princess Ivy
can't reach us.
But we're still **stuck!**

"I'll be back for the
amulet after I take over
your kingdom," Ivy says,
and then she's gone.

"Sofia, I'm sorry," Amber says. "I haven't been a very good sister. This is all my fault." I can't stay mad at her. "It's okay," I say. "But **how** are we going to get out of here?"

Suddenly, I notice my amulet **glowing. . . .**

There's a flash of light, and
Princess Rapunzel
appears!

"It looks like you two could use
a lift," she says with a smile.
"Climb on up."
She lowers her beautiful long
hair to help us climb out.
Then I tell her about Princess Ivy.
"How can we stop her?" Amber asks.

Just then, Everburn rushes
in with the singing dragons to take us
to the castle. As we ride, Rapunzel explains how to
break the curse: Amber must do something to prove
that I mean more to her than she means to herself.
We fly through a cloud, and when I look back,
Rapunzel is gone.

When we reach the castle, Ivy's coach is there, and everything is black and white. I hope we're not too late!

Oh, no!

Princess Ivy already zapped our family with
her dragonflies. Now she wants my amulet!
She sends a dragonfly toward me, but before
I know it—Amber jumps in front of it.

"Amber!" I cry. "Are you okay?"

"You should worry about yourself, Sofia," Ivy says,

tossing another a dragonfly at me.

But it flickers and disappears.

"What?" Ivy exclaims. "Why can't I..."

Her voice starts to fade—and then she does, too!

Amber let herself get
zapped to **save** me!
"This can't be!" Ivy cries, disappearing
in one last burst of sparkles as all
the color returns to the kingdom.
The curse is broken!

"What just happened?"
Dad wonders groggily.
Nobody remembers a thing
that happened today, thanks to those
dragonflies . . . which means the power
of the amulet is still a secret!

And now I know another secret . . .
Amber really is

the best
sister ever!

The End